It's a Wonderful Laura

Joni Järvi-Laturi

© 2021 Joni Järvi-Laturi
Kustantaja: BoD - Books on Demand,
Helsinki, Suomi
Valmistaja: BoD – Books on Demand,
Norderstedt, Saksa
ISBN: 978-952-804-369-0

PART I

SCENE ONE - THE SCHOOL

Laura is sitting while two wicked boys and one wicked girl throw
snus pieces on her back while laughing behind her.

The teacher is not present in the class.

Laura is suffering and thinking a way out.

LAURA
(thinking)
Public schooling should be made optional.
A forced educational duty to everyone doesn't belong
in the humanistic and intellectual spirit of the modern world.
Homeschooling is a divine option, the kid is supported by his or her
parents and doesn't experience the brutal and psychopathic bullying.
Homeschooling as an option to everyone would save millions of children
and young people into a kinder, gentler world. Public schooling is a joke,
an obsolete farce where everything is made to be a moral disgrace.
I want to tell my teacher about those three idiots who have bullied me
for three years. I can't wait vacation, the cruise ship, which is the only
place where I feel at home. I have no home. I am so fat and
I feel like crying myself to sleep. No, battle Laura, I know they have
humiliated you, but you must do something. Escape. Escape! I don't know
what to do. Maybe I should leave. Leave school for good. Escape from this
horrid society!

Laura attempts to leave the classroom.

The female teacher arrives at the door.

TEACHER
Where are you going, Laura?
You must attend school.

LAURA
Go away. I will never go to school again!
This is sick. I am bullied here!

The three wicked bullies laugh and the teacher
positions herself ahead of the class.

Laura leaves.

SCENE TWO – THE STREETS

Laura is walking the streets, with her hands in the pockets of her jacket.

NARRATOR
This is the story of a young woman. Her name was Laura, daughter of two entrepreneurs. Corpulent, heavy, at times only heavy-bodied, or proportionate. Se was shy and a bit sulky, yes, merciful, quiet and kind, almost always. She had a certain loneliness that was very close to a sense of solitude, without the pain, but there were people who were the barrier in front of the solitude, the enemies of her happiness, also in the mind of hers, but also in their random wickedness. Romantic, yes, she was introverted and romantic and she loved old Hollywood films and old pop music videos, as an escape from the world that was so chaotic and ugly. She reflected her thoughts on a diary, a red diary, which she had kept from the age of 11.

SCENE THREE – DINNER TABLE

Laura eats dinner with her mother and father.

FATHER
How are you, Laura?

LAURA
I am awaiting to go to the ship again.

FATHER
Oh, the cruise. That is such an important
place for you, has always been.

Laura's father smiles and looks satisfied.

MOTHER
Yes, by the way,
have you done your homework?

A flashback:
Suddenly Laura remembers her father
taking her to a spa when she was only 10
years old and very obese. She felt shame
about being so fat and remembered the
event tragically because she had a very low
self-esteem and saw her father's love for her

tragically touching because she was so lazy
and her father was so athletic. She pitied
both herself and her father back then.

LAURA
Yes I have.

MOTHER
Good, you must take the thrash out
and go to the post office. Remember?

LAURA
Oh, I had forgotten. I am a bit lazy
and gassy now.

FATHER
It's nice that you are so active.
This is exciting time for the family.

Laura glances at her father and
starts to think for herself.

LAURA
(thinking)
Father is such a nice man. Soft and innocent.
Thank you for everything, dear daddy. He never
suspects anything and is so proud of
this disappointment of myself.

Laura starts to cry.

LAURA
I have to leave now. Bye bye.

Laura's mother and father look at her,
crying.

Laura leaves.

SCENE FOUR - THE BRIDGE (EVENING)

Laura is walking on a bridge. She is smiling
but she is sad and bitter. She stops at the bridge
to look at passing cars driving ceaselessly and recklessly.
It is dark and the latter part of September, after
summer.

LAURA
The owners of the highways and roads.
They have a freedom to go anywhere.
Cars and more cars driving wildly like
victors of the world.

LAURA
Oh, this world is a nightmare. Everything is wrong.
Everything is upside down. So wrong.

Laura contemplates committing suicide
by jumping off the bridge. She stands to
face the cars but she decides against
suicide and watches the cars.

LAURA
Oh, lovely cars. You look so pretty.
You have saved my life.

LAURA
(thinking)
Why does everything mean
survive and everything gentle
lose? Do things settle themselves
in the future? The beauty of the soul,
the greatness of the heart. Why do
most people commit so many sins
not caring about them, evil words and
deeds like on an endless assembly line,
so selfish, thieves to thieves.
Most people are mean.
But then again, cars and jobs require
some meanness, I ponder. But there is still
the option, the option to be good.
I think I hate quarrels. They are
automatic cruelty for the people

by the people.

LAURA
(thinking)
We are the owners of the streets,
we walkers. My only right.
To be lost and getting lonely.
God, I wait for the ship.
Let's go Laura. Fight back!

Laura walks away from the bridge.

LAURA
God.

She exhales a deep breath, vividly
and excitingly.

SCENE FIVE – THE LIVING-ROOM

Laura sits with her sister, Maria,
as they watch television in the living-room.

MARIA
What do you want to watch, Laura?

LAURA
Nothing.

MARIA
Nothing?
Why nothing?

LAURA
This doesn't appeal to me.
This is not important.

MARIA
You should relax a little.

Suddenly Henry and John enter the living-room.
They are friends of Maria. They are young,
energetic and athletic, muscular men.

HENRY
Hi, Maria.

MARIA
Hi, you two. Busy day?

JOHN
Yes, a hard day as well.

HENRY
Is she going to leave?

MARIA
Who? What?

HENRY
Laura.

MARIA
Oh, yes, she is.

HENRY
Then would you please let her leave?
We have some serious things to talk to you.
No outsiders.

MARIA
Hey, Laura, would you please go to your room?
We have some talking to do.

LAURA
That is no excuse.

MARIA
Just leave.

Laura leaves the room feeling sad.

SCENE SIX - NIGHT CAR

Laura is sitting in a motionless car with
Maria who is on the driver's seat.

Maria glances at Laura cold-heartedly,
smiling meanly.

Maria starts to talk about Henry and John.

MARIA
You wouldn't believe what people say about you behind
your back, Laura. It is quite wild and wicked but you deserve it.
Why can't you stop being so quiet and withdrawn?
Start doing things more stylishly. You are so full of mistakes,
like a clumsy and unattractive harp. A drowsy, unkempt hobo.

LAURA
I knew that you would ceaselessly find faults in me.
Why are you so mean? Isn't there a better Maria than
what you are presenting to me? It is like I cannot be anywhere,
like I cannot breathe fresh, sympathetic people anywhere,

you are like a toxic breath, when bad breath makes people sad.
You treat me like I should always leave every place.
You love our non-relatives more than me, your little sister.
Shame on you!

MARIA
You really have some work to do, honey pie.

LAURA
Maria, you act a decent, good woman to everyone,
you like being seen as good even though you know
deep in your heart, that you are not good. A good person
wouldn't say those kinds of things to her younger sister.

MARIA
I have a right to say them, because you wouldn't understand
and improve if I didn't.

LAURA
You also fawn to strangers and local celebrities
like some kind of pathetic, talentless friend of theirs.
You never find faults in them, only me, the gentle one.

MARIA
Nobody is perfect, Laura. But I make fun of people
when they deserve it.

LAURA
What about John and Henry?
Are they perfect in your view?

MARIA
John said that you live and breathe ugliness.
And Henry discourteously said simply that you will never find the
man of your dreams if you don't work for yourself more.
He fears that you will be a bum, a sad person,
living in the streets.

LAURA
Oh, I always knew that they would wound me with that too.
What business is my life to yours if you just keep on attacking me?

MARIA
Well, I am more able to do things.
Like succeed in life. Or charm men. You can do neither.

LAURA
Yes, you were always the princess.
A perfect Cinderella, a woman without problems.

MARIA
Problems are for loser people.
I want to be a winner.

LAURA
What are you talking about?

MARIA
You'll see. You'll understand this in the future.

LAURA
Oh, God.

After thinking and watching to distance
Laura starts to cry and leaves the car.

Maria looks at her unemotionally with cold, cynical eyes
while she walks in the street.

SCENE SEVEN – THE TRAIN AND THE SUBWAY

Laura is on a train watching
landscape through the window
and writing her reflections to her red diary.

The train stops and then Laura takes a subway
and writes her thoughts there.

LAURA (O.S.)
I always loved going on a cruise ship away from my problems.
School was hell, people were hell, always selecting me for
the target of their senseless cruelty, which I always called a leech
and people were maggots and leeches, very primitive, offending
automatically, non-stop, pretending tolerance and discussion and
loving, and betraying themselves and lying to themselves about
the most basic moral questions, the centre of their humanity was
ignorance and cruelty and they defended themselves and their
favourite things with crushing violence even though they acted like
great people who were always better than everyone else. Now I
have a cruise ship ahead of me and I deserve my break from humanity
that doesn't deserve me.

SCENE EIGHT – THE CRUISE SHIP

Laura walks through the terminal.
She is tired and fed up but excited
about the trip.

Laura enters a cruise ship where there are
two thousand travellers. People are talkative
and happy everywhere.

Laura buys a lot of candies and potato chips and Coca Cola
from a shop.

Laura drinks Pepsi in a bar and plays a slot machine
without winning anything.

Laura goes to her cabin and relaxes. She is tired.
She falls asleep in her bed.

SCENE NINE – THE EMPTINESS

Suddenly the ship was empty.
There was nothingness everywhere.

Laura felt like a quiet and tender spirit
and her thoughts drifted along the silence.

Every floor was empty, what had happened?

Laura had a sense that this emptiness would last a long time.

She walked to an elevator and it went to eighth floor
where she took a deep breath and felt wonderful.

LAURA
(thinking)
These sliding doors. Poetic humming while
aloneness walks from place to place. I love it.
Maybe there are people somewhere, but I have never
felt such peace in this ship as now,
because there are no people. This is so very beautiful.

Her mind was inundated by past voices.
She felt joy and sorrow but joy won.

It took a hour as she walked the ship three times completely,
and the array of floors, stairs and corridors were walked over by her.

LAURA
(thinking)
I am a lonely soul, terrified of violence, hungry for goodness.
Aren't we all gentle souls like this? We fall in love with goodness,
we cherish goodness and we admire it like weaklings,
filled with shame of our own weaknesses and vulnerabilities.

LAURA
(thinking)
The annotated journals of Laura Wells.
I have drawn penises on my diary, I romantically
dream of an incessant shower bursting onto my cheeks.
I dream of lollipops, as I call them, penises. I feel aroused by
thoughts of being a whore, with someone spreading my
cheeks separating my legs and making love to me,
thoroughly and nicely, treating me with an

admiring respect at the same time. Chivalry is the best feeling,
a key to a door of womanly sensibilities, a passport of goodness
to enter heavenliness. And when I find my rose,
my pink lollipop, I love giving it pleasure, because the owner
of the lollipop is such a good and decent spirit that he
deserves his joy from me.

LAURA
(thinking)
I see curtains and mirrors, empty rooms.
This whole cruise ship is now empty,
like in a claustrophobic dream. The graveyard of the living.
Fortunately I have my highbrow literature here. Poetry and prose.
I feel like dancing while walking the whole ship around.
I feel so alone and it feels joyous.

NARRATOR
Suddenly Laura saw a man in the smoking lounge.
He was thin and looked ascetic and modest, about
45 years of age, experienced and humorous.
The man said hello to her and Laura was curious.

LAURA
Hey, who are you?

SMOKER
I am just passing by, a business trip.

LAURA
Sounds alluring.

SMOKER
It's nice in here.
What about you?

LAURA
Escape trip.

SMOKER
Okay, do you smoke?

LAURA
I have never smoked a cigarette.

It has never occurred to me to smoke a cigarette.
But can I have a taste of that cigarette that you are smoking?

SMOKER
Sure.

Laura starts to smoke a cigarette.

LAURA
This is tasteful. I have always loved the smell of cigarettes
but I have never smoked them.

SMOKER
Have you been here long?

LAURA
About two days.

SMOKER
Don't you find this funny that there
are no people here except us?

LAURA
I find it soothing and wonderful
even though I like people still.

SMOKER
Yes, it is quite peculiar still but I sympathize
with your feelings. I am an old man and I have never
been in a situation like this.

Laura glances at him, he looks peaceful and wise.
Laura respects him.

LAURA
I think we could be friends.

SMOKER
Yes, that would be nice. You seem like an interesting woman.

LAURA
(thinking)
Really? How fascinating that a man thinks

I am an interesting woman. I usually get attacked by
those weird male creatures verbally.
Thank God for kindness.

LAURA
Thank you. You seem like a good person.
I think that is important.

SMOKER
I know.

The smoker sheds his cigarette.

SMOKER
I love to think about the fields in
North Carolina and Virginia
while I smoke.

LAURA
Oh, dear God, that is so interesting!
That is a very beautiful thought!

SMOKER
I also have a lot of friends who like to
talk about cigarettes and cigarette news.
We have also watched cigarette films and
a couple of documentaries.

LAURA
That is so nice.

SMOKER
Yes, and the processing of cigarettes
in a factory also is greatly entertaining to watch.

LAURA
Yes, I have thought of the same thing.

SMOKER
Think about it, there are billion of us, smokers,
and some of us are being demonized just for the
fact that we like to put things to our mouths.
I also like Colas and never drink alcohol

but I consume Coke like I loved the processing
of them. I like to think about the magical world
of smoking, with all of its little details and intricacies
like I am a part of something ancient, some evergreen
pleasure that is traditional.

LAURA
I have thought of those same thoughts,
but you gave them lyrics.

SMOKER
Haha, do you like hamburgers?

LAURA
Yes I love hamburgers with cheese and onion.
I always feel special and awesome as I
buy a hamburger meal. But I still feel sorry for animals,
they are slaughtered too cruelly even to this day.

SMOKER
I know. Meat-eating makes the whole world
kin. It is like sex or sport or exercising. It is
difficult to think about a world without carnivores,
without meat industry. I have to say that I respect
the arguments of vegetarians and find them people
very admirable but I still love consuming meat products.

LAURA
I have the same disease or the same battle
which I cannot find a way out. I love meat.
I think I should start smoking. That smell is
charming, I have always been fond of it.

SMOKER
I know. I must go now. We can meet in this smoking room
in the next days as well. You are a good woman. Bye.

The smoker shows his fist. And he and Laura
hit their fists together as a symbol of solidarity.

LAURA
Bye, you dear man.

SMOKER
Bye, you nice woman.

SCENE TEN – BYPASSERS

The night sets outside the ship.

The morning weather
sets outside the ship.

Laura wakes up from her bed
in her cabin.

She goes walking the corridors
all the way to the lounge where
there is four seats near the window.

Laura sees two people, a man and a woman enter
the lounge where she is sitting, looking at the sea.

The man and the woman smile at Laura
and take a seat.

LAURA
Hi, who are you?

MAN
We are just by-passers,
on our way to business.

WOMAN
Business before pleasure.

LAURA
Ok, what business do you do?

WOMAN
We are botanists.

LAURA
That sounds interesting.
You are interested in plants?

WOMAN
Yes, we are.

LAURA
I wish there was an encyclopedia of flowers. I read
Wikipedia articles and they are a pleasure. I would buy
an extensive book about flowers.

MAN
There is no such book but there is an app in a cell phone
where one can recognize all flowers that one sees.

LAURA
Okay, nice. I used to let my brother to gather plants
for an assignment in school. I couldn't do it by myself.
I was too lazy and ignorant.

MAN
Okay, interesting. Maybe we should tell about this
to your former teacher.

LAURA
Haha, funny.

WOMAN
There are also animal and fish information
that one can read about from Wikipedia.

LAURA
Yes, books about those subjects would be nice as well.
Those are admirable and extensive books.

WOMAN
Yes, fish are remarkable creatures.

MAN
And animals are very interesting as well.

LAURA
Yes, I love them.

WOMAN
What is your favourite animal?

LAURA
I think squirrels and cats are the most divine,
the most sympathetic and beautiful.

WOMAN
Interesting. I like foxes and rabbits the most.

LAURA
It would be nice to know about birds more.

MIES
Yes, I am very inexperienced in that.
If I am with a bird catcher I feel ignorant.

LAURA
And then there is space. I ponder it.
Information doesn't go to my brain easily
when I read about facts and speculation about space.
But I hope that in the future I could consume it more easily.

MAN
One can go to a local astronomical association and watch the star sky
at nights with the help of a telescope.

LAURA
The speculation must be alluring and spell-binding.
To study the star sky and have fun at nights.

WOMAN
There are also associations for board games.

MAN
Chess and checkers.

LAURA
And films as well.
I am so young.
But this conversation
has helped me.
I must go now.

MAN
Thank you for your company.

WOMAN
Yes, thank you,
you are a nice young woman.

LAURA
Bye.

Laura leaves the lounge.

SCENE ELEVEN – 617

Laura stepped into a toilet and saw a note that was put on the mirror.
The writer was anonymous. Laura felt perturbed but excited. The note said:

"Dear young, lonesome woman in this empty ship, if you want to follow your
passion, the passion you have not yet experienced and realized, meet me at the room
617. Remember 617."

Laura looked at the note. She decided to walk to the room 617 right away.

As she walked the endless corridors to find that room, she felt like she was to
experience either heaven or hell. She hoped the experience would be something her
instinct told her - an unforgettable and important moment. She knew that she was the
woman that the note was talking about.

She enters the room 617 and notices that a man is standing there.

MAN
You must be Laura?

LAURA
Yes.

MAN
Have you had a nice trip?

LAURA
Nice, very nice. Who are you?

MAN
I won't divulge that information.

LAURA
Why do you know my name?

MAN
I only want to help you.
Do you trust me?

LAURA
Well, yes. It is rare that someone
wants to help me.

MAN
Soon, she'll be here.

LAURA
Who?

MAN
Susanna.

Five seconds later someone knocked the door.
Laura opened the door and there was
Susanna.

SUSANNA
Hey, Laura. I came here
as fast as I could.
How are you?

LAURA
Fine. Better. Slowly but surely.

SUSANNA
Well, great, Laura. I am here to help you.

LAURA
You too?

SUSANNA
Yes, listen.

LAURA
What?

SUSANNA
I want to give you
an extreme makeover, Laura.

LAURA
Why?

SUSANNA
Because you so deserve to be happy.

LAURA
How did you find me?
Where do you know me?

SUSANNA
We knew about you
before the trip.
We wanted to help you.

Susanna looked exhilarating, sunny, filled intensely passionate energy all around her body, like pools of freshly-squeezed orange juice flowing inside of her and falling through her energetic skin. Her liveliness was addicting.

Her hair was yellow and long, curly and aesthetic, while her face seemed to demand people to be divine, in a loving manner, a motherly attitude that charmed everyone around her. She was able to heal everyone and everything on planet Earth. She had lived a sexually liberated, free and joyous life so she understood men and women in a broad and tender manner.

Laura had scars on her face, because she was assaulted by a drunkard two years ago. That painful memory was reborn in her mind and she felt that Susanna was an antidote to that unfortunate feeling. The emotions of Laura were completely thankful and she finally noticed a human being who treated her openly with respect, as something divine and Laura loved the possibility of finding a place in the sun, never wanting to leave Susanna's presence.

Laura also thought that tantric healers were doing important work and were unfortunately disassociated from cold, frigid and puritan culture to the fringes, but

that would soon to be changed because the product, heaven inside everyone, was so
appealing, from the tyranny of modern society.

SUSANNA
Turn your back on me. Let me see your back.

LAURA
With pleasure.

Laura turns her back.

SUSANNA
Oh, I see some unfortunate burden on your back.
I can feel it. This is sad.

LAURA
Oh, but you can make it better, can you?

SUSANNA
Absolutely, honey. You're my sister.

LAURA
Okay.

SUSANNA
Now feel each touch of my hands as something warming,
as something perfect, to your wanting posture,
which hides your inner feminine greatness.

LAURA
Okay.

Laura closes her eyes and starts daydreaming.

LAURA
I feel tremendous emotions.
Your fingers are helping it to happen.

SUSANNA
I know it is so.
Just wait for the images and
emotion to come, the waves of
pleasure.

Then Susanna recommended
facial exercises to Laura and
cleansed her face with soft
lotions and then she washed
her hair with a hot water
and waxed it thoroughly.

LAURA
Oh, I feel so great!
Thank you!

SUSANNA
This is not over yet, honey.

LAURA
What is to come?

SUSANNA
Next there will be something
I call love dreaming, a way
to delve into the inner greatness
of Laura Wells.

LAURA
Sounds exciting.

SUSANNA
Do you like candies,
Laura?

LAURA
I like them a lot.

SUSANNA
I bet you do. You have eaten
a lot of candies and ice creams
and chocolates in your childhood.
I want to give you mind candy
or dream candy. Think of where
you are right now as I am massaging
your whole body, to the very end.

LAURA
I am on a shower, feeling my hair
being washed and soon I am going
to a film theatre.

SUSANNA
What is going to happen in the film theatre?

LAURA
I will perform in the movies.
I will step into a Western and
ride a horse with a woman,
with you.

SUSANNA
Very great, my sister!

LAURA
We both look relaxed and fruitful,
we look like we have been made love to,
from multiple men.

SUSANNA
Keep those lovely thoughts with you,
darling. I am your humble servant now.

LAURA
Now I am in a dressing-room.
There are numerous drag queens there
and they look fleshy and gay.
I want to pleasure them sexually.

SUSANNA
Interesting.

LAURA
I will walk to a street and meet a woman
and she is walking with me,
she needs money.

SUSANNA
This is your dark side.
The woman is intruding?

LAURA
Yes, she is. Now I am
on a train, just reading.
Oh, wait, now I am
in front of a rich family's
mansion, on the front yard,
and I stumble onto a patio.
I see a woman who is bathing
in the sun. I take a seat and
start to bathe in the sun myself
as well. Everything is idyllic
and heavenly. We are far away
from our problems.

SUSANNA
Great. Do you see your innocence,
your inner heaven, your heavenly
sexuality? Like you have just entered
a personal paradise? No more
bullying, no more depression,
no more tears?

LAURA
Yes, you read my thoughts!
You are a clairvoyant!

SUSANNA
I promise you that in the end
of this session you will have
the guts to live this heaven
for the rest of your life.

LAURA
Oh, thanks. Now I am
back in the desert with you,
my riding partner.

SUSANNA
Now, let me make a prediction.
You will meet a very similar,
like-minded female friend.

LAURA
How?

SUSANNA
You should wait for a day.
Then it will all be revealed to you.

After half an hour of session with Susanna,
Laura was tired and decided to go to her cabin and sleep again.
She was happy and she thought that something
was going to change.

SCENE TWELVE – THE DECK

Laura woke up in her cabin. She felt dizzy and tired
and felt like she hadn't slept enough.

After two hours of extra sleep she decided to start her day by going to the deck.

The ship was again full. There were two thousand people there and Laura felt
excitement and gratitude that there were people again, living a full life and enjoying
themselves. The difference between a full ship and an empty ship was palpable, and
Laura was surprised that the ship was yet again full.

Laura went to stand on the deck and smoked a cigarette there. She felt consolation
from the cigarette and considered it to be her best friend. The sea water rippled
attractively to her ear.

Two young females ran from far away on deck screaming and frolicking chaotically
until they saw Laura and stopped.

Their names were Milla and Jasmine.

Milla had an Eastern scarf, she was full of energy and talked a lot. She had red hair,
just like Laura had. She was 21 years of age. Jasmine had a black hair. She was tall
and skinny. She was more stern, reticent and quiet than Milla, but messed around
with Milla just like everyone would and enjoyed it.

MILLA
Who are you?

LAURA
My name is Laura.

What are you doing here?

JASMINE
We're just having fun.
Wanna join?

Laura looked at Jasmine a bit
but knew the answer instantly.

LAURA
Of course!

MILLA
Thank you, Laura!

NARRATOR
Laura, Milla and Jasmine ran in every floor three times
before they were exhausted. Milla had a tenacious,
stubborn vision to run the whole ship around, as outsiders,
with Jasmine and Laura and her exuberance and vivaciousness
irritated and bothered Laura a bit, Laura who didn't say about this
but kept it inside of hers. She said goodbye to the duo and went
to sleep again, quietly and peacefully.

SCENE THIRTEEN – THE HANGOVER

Laura woke up hung over from an inebriated night.
She was alone, while Milla and Jasmine were away.

She felt dizzy and decided to drink water from the bathroom faucet.

Suddenly she had a great urge to buy a cigarette carton and smoke a lot.

Laura walks away from a shop and carries a brand new cigarette carton to her room.

PART II

SCENE FOURTEEN – A FEMALE FRIEND

Laura is having a cigarette in a smoking lounge while a strong-looking, stern and intelligent woman arrives. She is called Silvia and she glances at Laura and Laura reminds her of her daughter. Silvia is 32 years old and she is a prolific writer with a sweet-tooth for whiskey. She is a brunette and quite long and thin.

SILVIA
What is your name?

LAURA
Laura is my name.

SILVIA
Ok, Laura.

Moment of silence.

SILVIA
Might we have a conversation
about something?

LAURA
About what? Cigarettes?

SILVIA
No, whiskey.
I like to talk about whiskey.

LAURA
Why?

SILVIA
I like to think about the life of whiskey.
The barrels, the barley, corn, rye, the fermentation, the distillation,
the people who make it, the very interesting people who consume it, the
whole business around it, the whole world around it, the rolling world,
where profit moves the drink into each continent and the secrecy and
the class behind it as well as the prohibited pleasure of it, that it is in a certain
sense forbidden to normal people who obey the rules. I like the glasses as well
and I like the bottles, each variety of whiskey is like a great surprise and selecting a
bottle to consume is always exciting, like receiving a present for Christmas.

LAURA
Tell me more.

SILVIA
There is South African whiskey, South American whiskey,
American whiskey, whiskey from Russia, whiskey from
Ireland, from different parts of Europe. I dig the advantageous
parts of whiskey, the dark, secret world of international commerce.

LAURA
Oh, that sounds so interesting!

SILVIA
I also like cigarettes.

LAURA
Ok, do you smoke cigars?

SILVIA
Yes, sometimes, I smoke them too little.
I am a bit of a bohemian artist, so
cigars suit me, though.

LAURA
What is your favourite season of the year?

SILVIA
I like the summer, it is the most lively and poetic.
I like the exciting youth sitting on grass and having fun.
I have so many warm, amazing memories about
the summer and the youth. Everyone is connected
to each other during summer and it is the season of love.

LAURA
What kind of an artist are you?
Do you like poets?

SILVIA
As a matter of fact I am a poet
and a writer. I like to write
intellectual and psychological
poems. I like to escape to different
realms of consciousness.

And I love a multitude of poets,
the classics, all the way from
Anne Sexton to W.B. Yeats
and Walt Whitman
and numerous others.

LAURA
I have always thought that different
poets have different personalities
that reveal themselves in the poems.
Everyone is different.

SILVIA
Yes, that is true, absolutely true.
I also love finding out what the words
and the idioms and the metaphors mean.
I like staring at the words but I also love
to solve the great poems like a mysterious
puzzle of the mind. At nights I study poetry
in a darkened room and I light the pages
with a flashlight. I also think about trees
as the books are manufactured and the plantation
of new trees and new books.

LAURA
That is great, fascinating.
You really are a writer.

SILVIA
Laura, shall we get drunk?
I need you as my partner.

LAURA
Absolutely Silvia.

SCENE FIFTEEN –
LAURA AND SILVIA AT THE CABIN

SILVIA
Hey, tell me something, Laura.
What are your interests concerning your future?
What do you want to be when you grow up?

LAURA
I think I want to do something creative,
leave my handprint in the world. I think I am
in a position where I don't completely know
what should I be and that is a blessing in a way.
But I have quite great writing skills and wouldn't
be surprised if I was a writer in the future.

SILVIA
Oh, a writer, one has to collect life experiences
for that, I can be your mentor, your mother figure
concerning honing your technique and finding your
artistic voice. It is a very great occupation, very
honorable as well.

LAURA
Yes, I know. What kind of life experiences
have you had? I'm curious to know.

SILVIA
Well, the last twelve years have been on my mind
most recently.

LAURA
You have thought of them, I see.
What happened during those twelve years?

SILVIA
Well, I lived and saw many foreign countries and experienced
living in Finland as a celebration of life, of local community and family.
I lived like no one else in the last decade. And during my stint
at the mental hospital the whole decade or twelve past years were
symmetrically put together, like 2008 and 2009 were some kind
of an opening without an ending, the mental wound I had was to be

put together. Everything just clicked, became symmetric,
like a miracle had happened. The psychiatric nurse, a male, had turned into my
friend, when twelve years before he said very mean things to me,
because I had acted very stupidly, and deserved his mean words. I saw my old school
bully as being quieter than me and turned into a shier, more vulnerable version of
himself. I also saw green men, men who were like big brothers, nurses and doctors at
the psychiatric facility, to reveal as being in their nature, green. It started when I was
a student at school, when I was 13 years old. A green-jacketed young boy bullied me
and I remembered him as being green. He was verbally very mean. In 2008 I
encountered a very fraternal man in the mental institution, he was like a big brother to
me. And the experience repeated itself in 2020. This was an incredibly mystical and
strange event.

The red men at the psychiatric facility, were more masculine, stronger than green
men, and the red men were at time offended by green men, perplexed and confused,
but the red men also had an advantage – they always beat the green men in social
situations, eventually, being stronger and more "real" men, like cowboys for
Marlboro, without anything weird or foreign or rare. The green men I guess where
more suave and cunning, but the red men had the physical force, not being thin like
green men. Like meat-eaters versus vegetarian-looking men.

I must say that I have travelled a lot but I don't remember anyone being a woman like
myself, talking about whiskey and cigarettes. I hope you, Laura, find this appealing
because you are the only one close to me. I find this funny. Even in the States I didn't
find anybody like me.

LAURA
You've been in the States?

SILVIA
Oh, yes, in 30 states.

LAURA
That's 20 missing. Which states were your favourites?
I'm very curious to know.

SILVIA
Well, first off, United States of America is such a great and large country with
profound ideals and great opportunities for many, many people, so all states are my
favourites. But I have to tell you that I fell in love with Texas and Ohio, even though
I am not a hillbilly, but more like a hippie. Still, the cities have progressed and
changed so rapidly and I love California as well. New York is powerful and always
filled with meaningful people. The greatness of America, or one of the greatness lies

in the numerousness of the states as well as the numerousness of cities combined with
the enormous amount of things found and the sophistication and plantation of each
section of society. It is a Western democracy, but it is a giant country filled with the
most interesting people and events as well. Even though I think Russians are the most
deep people, or the woman in there, I still think that Americans don't always
appreciate their country enough but are self-pitying themselves through their country
even though the country is mind-bogglingly awesome. All that food, drink and club
culture, as well as the versatile nature and miraculous buildings and historical sights
and details.

LAURA
Alright, you've given me enough information to chew.
I like thinking of what you say to me. What else
we should discuss?

SILVIA
I think I didn't mention enough about
poetry to you.

LAURA
What poet do you recommend?
I am frighteningly ignorant about
this issue.

SILVIA
I recommend many poets.
Langston Hughes is great
and simple, if you like jazz
and appreciate the struggles
of black people in American history.
Pablo Neruda is soft and he
writes about sea in a very complicated way
filled with liveliness. Anne Sexton
is interesting and has intriguing
confessions that have their quiet ambience,
like drinking coffee in a room.
W.B. Yeats is a peaceful poet, like
a gentle, old man whose poems are
like aspirin pills. Arthur Rimbaud
is difficult to understand but his poetry
is perhaps the greatest poetry in the world
when read in French language. He was a
great rebel but I still don't understand a lot from him.

LAURA
I must get to know those people.

They have a moment silence. Then Silvia breaks the ice.

SILVIA
Have you ever been in love, Laura?

LAURA
No, I haven't.

SILVIA
But let say you will. Say you meet some gorgeous man with a great body and a
fascinating mind, so I want to know, what kind of love you want to have with him,
how you caress him. And what kind of men do you seek? Are you a monogamist or a
bigamist?

LAURA
Oh, a difficult question. I think I am in between a monogamist and a bigamist. I also
like women by the way. I think I am a bisexual. I search for a good man who is easy
to please and who pleases me easily. I like penises and pussies and I liked that you
asked me a question about intimate pleasures. I would quite possibly satisfy him very
well because I am almost always interested in men's content behind their zipper. I
love giving pleasure to a woman as well, I am an oral woman, very oral, like you
seem to be.

SILVIA
Oh, I am an oral woman, absolutely. I like putting things in my mouth, like whiskey,
cigarettes and penises.

They both laugh.

SCENE FIFTEEN –
THE DRUNKEN MUSINGS OF LAURA WELLS

Laura sat on the floor of the cabin as Silvia danced
elegantly to Yemenite and Turkish songs. Laura
admired the bohemian and deeply mysterious
rapier wit of Silvia. Laura loved her new friend
who was her big sister and protector in some
way and admired how Silvia was sharp as a tack.

LAURA
(drunk, thinking)
The chairs, the corridors, the doors, the suites!

I think I must now ponder what kind of a woman I am and what kind of niceties
enflame my womanhood. This is not a shy notion, but more like a lyric literature of
the mind. The cunt confession.

I am attracted to a strong and silent guy who is also kind. I like the changes of
perception that happen when meeting a new mind and discovering daring dimensions
of a life that gives me pervasive perspective, a feeling of novelty. The mother-in-
laws, the sister-in-laws, the feeling of power within the family that has a bit of
communal fun together. I also like a sense of ubiquitous manhood, a feeling of all-
around testosterone floating through-out my body like roaring gasoline.

If I was an empty sheet of paper my man would nail new rules for me with a punctual
typewriter. I like the thought of two people exploding like an alarm clock with their
penis and vagina.

I have breasts that are big, to entice the right man. I love carrying my tits, my ass and
my vagina with my tough and spirited body. They are my personal rewards for the
man who will love me. I am also proud of my pubic hair, a primitive, strong and
earthly pleasure for a man who misses motherly qualities in a woman. I also like a
man being weaker at times and wanting to cuddle under my arms. Maybe I will grow
up to be a rambunctious, adventurous, slightly masculine lady who does manly things
as well as feminine things.

I loved the way Silvia talked about different countries as I asked her about them. She
eloquently and emphatically gave me tour of each country, what an intelligent

woman! She knows one hundred countries and gave great data concerning them – I was amazed!

Now I must go to the night. The vacation is over tomorrow, an end of an era. I cannot think of anything to say or do anymore. Soon I will pass out after I have exhausted this ship and all its contents, and savagely and gluttonously eaten everything it has offered to me.

SCENE SIXTEEN – WAKING UP

Laura wakes up.

She brushes her teeth and drinks water.

She thinks of Silvia, who is not present.

FLASHBACK
SILVIA
What interests you, Laura?

LAURA
Deep, extreme conversations and periods of extreme consciousness.

SILVIA
So, you are like a man, like I am. Little sister. Little bird of mine.
It is often thought that LSD, whiskey and psychedelics, hunting and deep, extreme stuff is the area of men.

LAURA
Yes, I find that to be the common stereotype.

SILVIA
It is strange, very strange, but a very common interest of men.

LAURA
I also like greatness in music, films and literature.

Two angels are standing in heaven.
They look at what Laura is doing
in the empty ship and speculate over
her.

1st ANGEL
It is funny how people act down there
where we don't have to. This game is
entertaining to watch.

2nd ANGEL
What do you think of her?

1st ANGEL
Laura? Well, she is blooming.
Soon she doesn't need help much.

2nd ANGEL
But we are going to meet her still.

1st ANGEL
We must say a couple of things
to her. She is so innocent and
lively right now.

2nd ANGEL
Yes, she makes me happy.
I wonder what will happen
after she leaves the ship.

1st ANGEL
Let us hope for the best.

2nd ANGEL
She is so literal,
so intelligent.
She will burst into a
great flower.

1st ANGEL
Yes, I want her to flourish.
Like a nightingale singing,
like a squirrel running,
like sunflower blooming.
Oh, how I want her to flourish.

**The two angels descend onto Earth,
onto the ship where Laura is having**

a moment of melancholy in her room.

They walk the corridor at the ship. Soon, they find Laura's cabin and
they knock on the door. Laura opens the door and is amazed at the two strangers.

LAURA
Who are you?

2st ANGEL
We are two angel spirits.

LAURA
Oh, oh, okay.
What are you doing here?

1st ANGEL
Laura, we are the guardians of your greatness,
the angels of your admiration.

LAURA
No one has ever spoken to me that way.

The angels smile at Laura.

LAURA
But what do you do here?

2nd ANGEL
We want to move you closer to your destiny.
and nearer to your beauty.

LAURA
How so?

1st ANGEL
You have been mourning over meanness
of your brutal past. We are here to tell you,
Laura, how great your future is going to be.

LAURA
How?

2nd ANGEL
The men, the wicked men in your life, well this is
what they actually said in your absence.

The angels touch Laura's hand and Laura starts to hear men
talking about him while has been away at the cruise.

LAURA
Is it good?

The angels smile to Laura.

1st ANGEL
Just listen, darling, carefully.

Laura sees Henry in her mind, talking about her.

HENRY
(in a vision, thinking out loud)
"We are allies, me and Laura. I hope I haven't hurt her.
God, how I hope she would find true love in her life,
I feel sorry for her because everyone bullies her about
her weight. I hope she would be happy, like I am. Her lovely
opulence. Her kind, smiling eyes, her glad, glistening lips.
She represents the victory of both mind and body over hideous prejudice."

LAURA
Oh, God.

JOHN
(in a vision, thinking out loud)
"God, I feel sorry for Laura. I think about where she
might be now. I hope she is not crying. She has such
beautiful mind and great soul and I wish that she would hear this
that I admire both her soul and her physical beauty. She makes
me a better person. After every time I meet her,
I think that she only thinks good and kind thoughts, always.
That is such an admirable characteristic. The decency of a great lady.
How could she forgive me?"

Laura is surprised and starts to smile.

1st ANGEL
You see, Laura, we all want the absolute best for you.

LAURA
How lovely. I am positively surprised. Thank you.

1st ANGEL
What are you thinking right now, Laura?

LAURA
I am thinking about my leaving from this beautiful ship.
Laura was here. I guess that's good.

2nd ANGEL
Do you leave the ship thinking about your
misunderstood womanhood?

LAURA
I never thought men would be so kind to me.
Those men, who I have thought of so crude.

1st ANGEL
Our job is done. Thank you.

The angels leave the room smiling to Laura.

SCENE SEVENTEEN – LAURA'S RETURN

Laura is walking in a group of people
on the terminal to exit the ship.

Laura comes back to her family's house.

She watches hockey in the living-room
with Henry and John.

Henry asks her how was the trip.

HENRY
Well, how was it?

LAURA
With merry thoughts and dreams I departed the ship when in anguish and misery I
arrived at it. Dreaming of a man, a gentle and tender man, in my bed, in my cabin, a
lover who never crosses the street where two lovers hate to leave each other. I
reconciled the fact that there was not a romantic soul outside ship in my life, only
chaotic people, extroverted and gregarious, willing to be in deep contact only with the
worst of human traits, profane and sickening immorality. I sank into deep sleep,
while the ship was rolling its impersonal and forgettable trip and only in the pictures
of thousand cell phones was the legend of the trip, the duration of it, eternalized.

HENRY
But we men, we your friends, we were thinking of you Laura, the materialization of
your well-being. Our eternally loving thoughts were a tribute to you, Laura.

LAURA
I know. Two angels spoke to me. That is when I knew I was beloved and blessed.
I have started to understand men more and enjoy my womanhood more. Oh, how I
love that it is Christmas now. The winter has been frigid and cold, I have feared
cynical folks but now I am filled with the spirit of Christmas. To give and to receive,
I guess that is what makes the sacred time of the year so special.

HENRY
Oh, what a nice surprise, Laura.

LAURA
I like your lips, Henry. I hope I will have a taste of them someday.
Now I am busy, but we will see each other, won't we?

HENRY
Anytime, Laura. Anytime.

FINAL SCENE

Laura arrives at her family's house where her mother Lisa and her father
Timothy are celebrating the Christmas with Laura's sister Maria.

LAURA
Oh how I have missed you all!
Come here and give me a hug!

Laura hugs her sister and her parents.

LISA
You are so beautiful, Laura!

LAURA
Oh, thank you.

MARIA
Forgive me as I was so cold to you,
Laura. I hate myself for what I said
to you.

LAURA
It's okay, it's Christmas, Maria.

TIMOTHY
You seem so happy, are you happy, Laura?

LAURA
I am, father, very happy, indeed. And at last I have found the
gift of Christmas and the wait for a New Year makes me so satisfied.
Thank you to all you folks!

THE END